CANDY Claus ®
THE
NEWEST MEMBER OF SANTA'S FAMILY

An Original Story Created by LOUIS CORBO

Adapted by JOAN CHASE BOWDEN

Illustrated by AL LOWENHEIM

Oak Tree
San Diego, California

On Christmas Day at the North Pole, Santa Claus sat snoozing in front of a cozy fire. What a busy Christmas Eve it had been, delivering toys to all the children. Between snoozes, Santa wondered if the boys and girls had liked the gifts he'd left for them.

Suddenly there was a knock on the front door. Mrs. Claus hurried to answer it, then couldn't believe her eyes! There, sitting in a tiny sleigh on Santa's own front porch, was the prettiest doll she had ever seen. A note attached to it said:

To: SANTA CLAUS
From: THE CHILDREN OF THE WORLD
We hope you love this doll as much as we love you!

When Santa saw his beautiful present, he was so surprised! He cradled the doll in his arms. But even he didn't expect what happened next! All at once, the doll grew warm. Her eyes brightened. Then she stirred to life!

hank you both for bringing me into your home," she said. "I was so cold outside in my little sleigh."

Santa and Mrs. Claus were astonished! They knew that something very special had just happened. So strong was Santa's love for the children of the world, and so strong was their love for Santa, that the little doll had turned into Santa's real-life child!

$\mathcal{H}$o-ho-ho!" Santa chuckled. "So now we have a new member of the family. But what should we name her?"

Before Mrs. Claus could answer, the little girl reached for a candy cane. "I've got it!" Santa said. "She likes candy canes, so that's what we'll call her— CANDY CLAUS."

Mrs. Claus thought it was a beautiful name.

In the weeks that followed, little Candy Claus became a treasured part of Santa's family. She helped make cookies in the kitchen.

She helped tidy papers in the study.

ut the place where she liked most to help was Santa's workshop. Every afternoon she helped the elves test the toys, just to make sure they worked. And every afternoon, always by accident, she broke some!

"Oh dear," said Elfie the foreman. "If things go on like this, the toys will never be ready for Christmas."

Then Elfie had a wonderful idea. He had the elves make the little girl a doll of her very own to play with.

"This will keep Candy out of our workshop," Elfie said.

andy loved the doll. It looked like a big gingerbread cookie, so she named it Ginger and took it with her everywhere. She took it to the kitchen.

She took it to the study.

She took it to Santa's workshop every afternoon! The elves didn't know what to do! But Santa knew what to do. There would be no toys this Christmas if the elves couldn't get on with their work. So he painted a big sign.

And he pinned it on the workshop door. It said: PLEASE KEEP OUT! When little Candy Claus saw the sign, she was very upset.

ig tears rolled down her cheeks. "Oh," she sobbed. "How could Santa shut me out from his workshop? I was only trying to help."

She even began wondering if Santa and Mrs. Claus had really wanted a little girl of their own after all. Candy was so upset that she grabbed Ginger and ran outside. She ran and ran across the snowy fields until she could run no more. Then suddenly, she stopped and looked around her. Santa's little house was nowhere in sight!

At that very moment, a terrible storm blew across the North Pole. The wind howled. The snow fell. Soon Candy felt cold and frightened and unloved—and lost!

It wasn't long before everyone at Santa's house realized that Candy was missing. The elves looked everywhere.

"Oh," cried Mrs. Claus. "Where can she be?"

Santa was worried as he climbed into his sleigh "I won't rest until I find her," he said, heading into the terrible storm.

What a blizzard it was! Santa searched for hours for his little girl. Then suddenly, he saw something sticking out of a snowbank. It was Ginger! And lying right beside her was his own Candy Claus. But she was cold and still. Thinking that no one loved her, Candy had turned back into a doll!

Santa held her close. "Oh, Candy," he cried. "Please come back to us. We all love you very much."

At once he felt her grow warm in his arms. She stirred and sat up. "Do you really love me?" she whispered.

Santa hugged her to his heart, glad that once more his love had brought her to life. They were so happy as they flew home in Santa's sleigh.

What a celebration there was when they returned!

"Don't ever leave us again," Mrs. Claus whispered to her little girl. "We couldn't live without you now."

Then Santa told everyone his big surprise. "We all know that Candy wants a job of her very own," he said. "So from now on, she will look after the baby reindeer."

WELCOME HOME CANDY !

andy thought it was the best job in the
whole world! Santa introduced her to
Snowflake, whose little nose somehow always wore one.

Next came Sleighbell who jingled when he walked. Then Candy met Winter, whose coat was cold but whose heart was warm. And last was Mistletoe, who liked kissing—especially Candy. He licked her face gently to show that he loved her too.

When it was almost Christmastime, kind Elfie made Candy a little sleigh so that she and her young reindeer could practice their flying lessons every day. Soon they were flying all around the North Pole. How proud Santa and Mrs. Claus felt as they watched them!

Then, on Christmas Eve, Candy had a wonderful idea of her own. "Now that my baby reindeer can fly," she told Santa, "I can deliver my candy canes in my own little sleigh!"

Mrs. Claus was worried. It was a big job for such a small girl. But Santa chuckled as he climbed into his big sleigh loaded with toys.

Santa picked up his reins and called, "On Dasher! On, Dancer! On, Prancer and Vixen! On, Comet!, On, Cupid! On, Donner and Blitzen!"

Candy picked up her reins, too. She called, "On, Snowflake! On, Winter! On, Sleighbell and Mistletoe!" Santa's sleigh rose high into the sky.

But, as Santa had known all along, Candy's reindeer had never before practiced with a loaded sleigh. They pulled and they tugged, but they simply couldn't budge it.

Santa smiled as he flew back to Candy's side. "It was a wonderful try," he said. "This time I'll take the candy canes. But won't you try again next year?"

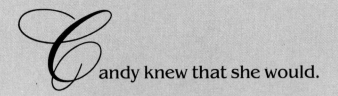

Candy knew that she would.